I Have Two Moms

by Colleen LeMaire

Illustrated by Marina Saumell

For Ellen, who paved the way for acceptance,
inclusion and a world based on kindness.

To Jessica and Megan...brand new Moms who found
the time to help make sure I got this one right.
Thank you.

Lastly, to my husband. For believing in me, encouraging
me to never give up on my dreams, and for loving our life
together the way that you do. Even when we're caught
in a storm, you always find the rainbow.
You are my person, and I love you so much.

Once upon a time, I was born.
I was the cutest, cuddliest baby
in the whole world, and my parents
couldn't wait to take me home.

I live here, with my parents.
I have two Moms,
and I love them
with my whole heart.

Growing up, I've learned families come in lots of different shapes and sizes.

Some kids live with a Mom and Dad.
Some live with grandparents.

I have friends that live with an aunt and uncle, and others that take turns between their Mom's house and their Dad's house.

Homework:
My Family

Grandma

Grandpa

me

Some have two Dads,
or two Moms, like me.

My family looks like this.
Me, and my Moms.
I call them Mom, and Mama.

Sometimes kids ask me where my Dad is,
and it can be confusing for them to understand.

I do my best to explain that all families look
different, and each family member feels
and gives love in their own special way.

I am lucky enough to have two Moms
that love each other very much.
After they decided to spend their lives together,
they both really wanted to start a family.
That's where I came in!

My Moms take care of me.
They make sure I eat healthy.

They help me do my homework.

They always make sure
I get an extra scoop of ice cream
when we go to the carnival!

...g to do with my parents
...ght. My moms let me eat
... as I want!

My favorite thing to do with my Mom is play hide and seek. I always win!

My favorite thing to do with my Mama
is to go for a bike ride. We love
getting outside and enjoying nature!

My family is perfect just the way we are.
Having two Moms means my heart
is full of love, and love is all you need
to have a family.

My Moms will always love me,
they will always take care of me,
and they will always be there for me.
Pinky Promise.

About the Author

Colleen was catapulted into the world of parenting when she fell in love with a handsome single Dad. Like any parent, she has experienced the trials and triumphs of raising a child over the years, and says the journey has brought her a level of happiness she didn't know existed.

She is a loving Stepmom to her young stepdaughter, who sparked her passion to create a children's book series for all types of families. Colleen currently lives in the Chicagoland area with her husband, whom she says makes the crazy ride of parenthood all worth it.

Published by Colleen LeMaire
Printed in the United States of America.

Illustrated by Marina Saumell

ISBN: 978-1077909434